Thomas A. Richards

Miller's Guide to Saratoga Springs and Vicinity

Volume 1

Thomas A. Richards

Miller's Guide to Saratoga Springs and Vicinity
Volume 1

ISBN/EAN: 9783337368883

Printed in Europe, USA, Canada, Australia, Japan

Cover: Foto ©Andreas Hilbeck / pixelio.de

More available books at **www.hansebooks.com**

MILLER'S

GUIDE

TO

SARATOGA SPRINGS

AND VICINITY.

Illustrated.

BY

T. ADDISON RICHARDS.

NEW YORK:

PUBLISHED BY JAMES MILLER,

522 BROADWAY.

1867.

CONTENTS.

SARATOGA.

TOPOGRAPHY.

THE little village of Saratoga, where dwells the benign goddess Hygeia in the midst of her far-famed waters of life and health, is most pleasantly hidden within the heart of a broad stretch of varied table-land, in the upper part and near the eastern boundary of the great State of New York. The location is not remarkable for natural beauty, yet its immediate surroundings are by no means without attractions, while within easy reach, all about, may be found many of those beautiful landscape scenes for which the Empire State is so justly renowned.

The village, while most agreeably secluded from, is yet within the easiest and speediest reach of the busy world around. It is large enough to boast of a fixed population of some seven thousand, which may be trebled in summer-time by foreign incursion; and it possesses in abundance all the many ways and means of convenient and pleasurable life, in a liberal furniture of churches, schools, stores, shops, and all other appointments of home and social ease and comfort; with all of which it still retains that quiet country aspect, so grateful always to the eye and heart of the wearied *forçat* escaping from the galleys of Fashion and of Trade, and seeking the recuperating quiet and repose of country life. Even the most thronged portions of the village, where stand the great summer hotels, the flaring emporiums of the city modes, and all the transient glare and glitter of congregated fashion, are gratefully tempered by the screening and cooling shade of verdant trees: while reaching far around this more busy region, stretch long avenues of picturesque cottages, interspersed agreeably with more stately villas and manorial homes.

It is a healthful region, within the reach and influence of mountain airs, and is desirable, in this respect, as a summer abode, even apart from the great resource in its exhaustless mineral fountains. Pleasant roads also lead outward in all directions to still pleasanter resorts, as we shall see in other divisions of our story—roads not so faultless to be sure as the well-graded and hardened drives of the Central Park; for the soil is sandy, and has, at best, its ups and downs: as, indeed, country roads should have, to maintain their proper rural spirit. It may be all very well for the professional tourist to reach the summit of Mount Washington or the icy crest of Mont Blanc by the time-table and the rail; but where in that case is the old traditional and natural romance and adventure of country life and travel? In the near neighborhood of Saratoga are the upper waters of the beautiful Hudson, yet fresh and bright from their mountain cradles, not far away. Hard by, in another direction, flows the gentle Mohawk, through placid and fruitful meadows and plains. Many other picturesque streams dance amidst the region, and numerous sweet lakes and lakelets lie around. Within the range of a pleasant excursion are the great waters of Champlain, and equally accessible are the smaller but more lovely floods of Lake George, while yet beyond stretches the great wilderness of the Adirondack, with its weird lakes and its rock-ribbed hills,—to this day, a terra incognita, scarcely invaded by human habitation, and abounding in all its ancient stores of game, in beast, and bird, and fish, from the wary trout to the lordly moose—profuse even to the disgust of the scientific Walton or Nimrod, who needs the intervention of difficulty to give zest to his sport.

With so many, so varied, and so pleasant surroundings, the summer resident at Saratoga will be at no loss, when the dust of fashion gathers too thickly about him, to shake it off at intervals, in more quiet and secluded haunts: returning from a day's, or even a few hours' excursion, with renewed life and invigorated spirits.

HISTORY.

There is very little doubt that the mineral waters of Saratoga were well known to the aboriginal inhabitants, long before they were visited by the white men, and that they employed them as remedial agents, with the same intuition which they have ever displayed in their discernment of the virtues of the herbs and trees of their native wilds. To be sure they subjected the brooks to no scientific analysis, and knew nothing of a sodand sodium, of lime, or magnesia, of hydrogen or oxygen, or of the thousand and one unpronounceable diseases to which the waters gave relief: but they nevertheless always adapted the cure to the complaint as effectually as the most learned Esculapius of our own wise age. We may imagine the unctuous "ugh" of content or of disgust,—according to taste,—with which some antediluvian "Hole-in-the-Day" bent down in the primeval woods, and, pushing aside the weeds and snakes, won an appetite for breakfast from the stimulus of the bubbling brook. The scene must have been more picturesque, though may-be less comfortable, than that now presented of the beaux and belles daintily touching the crystal goblet with gloved fingers, or guarding their silken robes, as they drink, from the dampness of the tessellated marble floors.*

The Springs first became known to the European settlers in the latter part of the last century, when they were visited by Sir William Johnson, then in the service of the British government. This was in the year 1767. Sir William, who held at that period a major-general's commission under his majesty George III., had two years before defeated the French forces under the Baron Dieskau, at the battle of Lake George. In this engagement he received a severe wound, from which, at intervals, he was ever afterwards a great sufferer. It was to alleviate the pain of these attacks that he followed the counsels of some friendly Mohawks, and determined to visit the Springs. His worthy name was thus that of the first Euro-

---

* The author, in the "Knickerbocker Magazine," October, 1859.

pean ever entered upon the visitors' record at Saratoga. Of course he did not travel by rail, as we do to-day, or by post, as did our great-grandmothers, but through the bush and brake of the wild Indian trail, as best he could ; neither did he find shelter under the broad and hospitable roof of any Union or Congress Hall, but rested his weary limbs beneath the shelter of his simple forest tent only. Unhappily, he did not benefit himself by his visit so much as he did the thousands who have since followed his valuable guidance.

In Mr. William L. Stone's admirable "Life and Times of Sir William Johnson" we are told the valiant baronet, "accompanied by his Indian guides, set out on his journey on the 22d of August, and, passing down the Mohawk in a boat, soon reached Schenectady. At this place, being too feeble either to walk or ride, he was placed on a litter and borne upon the stalwart shoulders of his Indian attendants through the woods to Ballston Lake. Tarrying overnight at the log-cabin of Michael McDonald, an Irishman who had recently begun a clearing on the shores of the lake, the party plunged again into the forest, and following the trail of Indian hunters, along the shores of Lake Saratoga and its chief tributary, the Kayaderosseras, reached their destination."

The particular spring of which Sir William drank, was that very remarkable one now known among the numerous group as the High Rock ; and which must therefore receive the honors of, and be duly respected as the venerable father of this mighty family of magic waters.

The period of Sir William's visit to the High Rock, it will be seen, was that of the famous war in this region

2

between the French in Canada and the English below the St. Lawrence, and their Indian allies on either side. Forts had been erected, and settlements made at various points through the region, as far north as Lake George, but the troublous state of the country forbade any very rapid or permanent colonization, until the tomahawk was finally buried and the pipe of peace was smoked.

It was not until the year 1773, six years after Sir William Johnson's initial visit, that the first clearing was made and the first cabin erected at the Springs. The hardy adventurer who accomplished this brave feat was Derick Scowton. He commenced business in the double capacity of hotel-keeper and Indian trader. Unluckily, matters did not thrive between bold Derick and his red neighbors, who made his new home so unpleasantly hot that he found it wise to abdicate, leaving his hotel incomplete.

Derick was followed a year later, and with better success, by George Arnold, an adventurer from Rhode Island. Arnold took possession of the vacated Scowton House, and "ran" it, as we say at this day, with tolerable success, for about two years. How many daily arrivals he had is not upon the record, neither does history enlighten us in respect to his bill of fare, or his per diem. Still, it is clear that neither one nor the other in any way approached the Leland "ideas" of our day.

The third Saratoga landlord was one Samuel Norton, who squatted on the Scowton estate soon after the exit of George Arnold. Norton made various improvements, clearing and cultivating the land around him. He might have made a "good thing" of his enterprise, but, as ill-luck would have it, the first mutterings of the great storm of the Revolution just then began to greet his terrified ears, causing him to decamp, and thus leave the Hotel Scowton again without a landlord. Norton was at length, in the year 1783, succeeded by his son, who, taking possession of the old property, still further improved it, until 1787, when he sold out to Gideon Morgan, who in his turn and within the same year made it over to Alexander Bryan.

Bryan became the first permanent settler at the Springs after the close of the war. He enriched the estate with a blacksmith's shop and an additional log-house.

The days of the Scowtons, the Arnolds, the Nortons, the Morgans, and the Bryans were the primitive days of very small things; indeed the first or exploratory epoch in the settlement of the spring region. They were followed in 1789 by a new and more brilliant era, under the reign of the Putnams—an era and reign which steadily advanced from that hour, and has continued, ever expanding, down to our own days of full fruition.

Gideon Putnam is deservedly remembered as the father of Saratoga, by virtue of the many and varied contributions which he made to the growth and prosperity of the village, from his first settlement in it, in his early youth, to his death, twenty-three years later. He was a Massachusetts man, who set out in quest of fortune in the spirit of indomitable energy which he never afterwards failed to display in all his many undertakings.

He reached Saratoga, or rather the site of the present village—for the region was then still a wilderness in the year 1789. Before reaching this his permanent and final abode, as it afterwards proved to be, he wandered far through the wilderness, making various unsatisfactory attempts to enshrine his household gods. He first pitched his tent and built a hut in Vermont, on the spot now occupied by Middlebury. Later he established himself in Rutland. From Rutland he moved on to the "Five Nations," or "Bemis Flats;" and from thence he made his final journey to the forest land, now traversed by the streets of Saratoga. The first occupation of the hardy pioneer in his new home was of course to erect a cabin to shelter himself and his family, for the locality boasted no furnished houses to let at that period. He next leased some three hundred acres of land, which he set about clearing and cultivating. Soon after he erected a mill, by means of which he sawed lumber, which he sold in New York—realizing from it the means of still further advancing his improvements at home. Step by step he laid the foundations of his village, and step by step saw it grow and thrive, until in the year 1802, only thirteen years after his first sight of the spot as a wilderness, he commenced the erection of the building since so familiarly known as "Union Hall," and now one of the most spacious and popular hotels in the land.

It is said that Putnam's ambition, from early youth, was to build himself a "great house;" and though that portion of the Union Hotel which he erected—some seventy feet in extent—was but a small part of the present edifice, still it was a mammoth structure for its day and location. Putnam afterwards commenced the building of that other spacious structure opposite the Union, the late Congress Hall. While the masons were at work on the piazza of the Congress, he was walking upon the scaffolding, which gave way, and precipitated him and others on to the rocks and timbers beneath, breaking some of his ribs and otherwise so injuring him that he never fully recovered from the effects.

It is to the enterprise and industry of this hardy founder that Saratoga is indebted, more than to all others put together, not only for her general improvement at this stage of her history, but for the development and utilization of her mineral waters. One after the other, he excavated and tubed the principal fountains, and put them in that condition which has in due time won for them their world-wide renown. He died on the first day of December, 1812, and was the first person buried in the cemetery which he had himself presented to the village.

The famous hotel of Union Hall, erected by Gideon Putnam, was conducted by himself and his descendants, almost to the present day. The period of its history—from the early time when it displayed the sign of " Put and the Wolf," to the recent day when it passed out of the conduct of the family, and had grown too stately to bear any sign at all—is the period of the growth and maturity of the village and its present enviable fame. The further history of Saratoga may be better read in our proposed glance at the various scenes and objects of interest, as we may meet with them in our rambles over the village and its vicinage.

ROUTES TO SARATOGA.

Sir William Johnson, the first white visitor at Saratoga, had, as we have already said in our brief historical chapter, considerable difficulty in finding his tedious way thither, through forest and dell, with no better guidance than a

2*

blind Indian trail. Happily for us, the roads have been somewhat improved within the hundred years that have gone by since the valiant baronet made his fashionable tour.

Now-a-days, instead of blazing the forest-trees as we go, we blaze along, thirty miles per hour, upon the endless, irresistible rail, and in the interval between breakfast and dinner reach our destination from points hundreds of miles removed. Our journey, too, from whatever direction, may be as pleasant as it will be speedy, carrying us, as it will, through some of the most picturesque scenery in the land.

From New York we reach Saratoga via the charming passage of the lordly Hudson, which we may follow by rail along its banks or on the decks of one or other of the sumptuous steamers which ply the broad waters by day and by night. The hours of travel in this direction will fly fast enough, in the contemplation of the varied and striking scenes which will arrest the eye at every step—the rugged flanks of the Palisade, the great Tappan Sea, the cliffs and crags of the Highlands at West Point, the beautiful Bay of Newburgh, the long ranges of the Catskills, and the endless succession of cities, towns, and villas which everywhere bedeck the shores. Rightly to enjoy this part of the trip, the tourist should provide himself with Miller's "Illustrated Guide to the Hudson," recently published in a style uniform with our present volume.

On reaching Albany or Troy, the tourist will continue and complete his journey by rail. The whole distance from New York to the Springs is about two hundred miles, the time six hours, and the fare about three dollars and a half.

The readiest route is by Troy, where the change from one railway to another is made without trouble in the *same* *depot*. The crossing of the river at Albany involves some care, and, perchance, confusion to the uninitiated.

Before this volume is published it is most likely that the new railway route, via Athens, on the Hudson, will be opened. This will be a better way from New York to the Springs than any other. Passengers may leave the Metropolis in the night-boats, and landing at Athens, some thirty miles below Albany, take the cars, and be at Saratoga in good season for breakfast.

From Boston the route is direct, two hundred miles, via the Western Railway to Albany, and thence as from New York. The journey, though rather long for one day's work, is an interesting one. It leads through the entire length of Massachusetts, calling at Wooster and Springfield and Pittsfield, and traversing much of the beautiful mountain region in the northwestern part of the old Bay State. Taken in instalments it would be pleasant enough ; but the old saying, " too much of a good thing," etc., is always painfully verified in railway travel, no matter how picturesque may be the region through which one is passing.

Another and perhaps better route from Boston, is via Fitchburg and Bellows Falls.

From Buffalo and the West, Saratoga is quickly reached by the route of the Central Railroad to Schenectady, and thence via Ballston Springs. It 's a pleasant though a long journey, and affords a peep at many important cities and towns and at much picturesque landscape.

From Montreal and other northern points, the traveller may reach the Springs via Lake Champlain to Whitehall,.

and thence by rail; or he may leave the lake at Burlington, and make the rest of his way by the Vermont railroads.

NOMENCLATURE.

Saratoga is an Indian word of the dialect of the Iroquois. The inflection *oga* at the end is said to mean place, while the *Sa-ra*, or, as it is otherwise written, *Sar-at*, and again *Sar-agh*, is supposed to be equivalent to salt,—making the original designation, Saraghtoga, to mean the place of salt springs. Again, it is by other Indian scholars supposed that Saragh means herrings—and thus the whole word, " the place where herrings are caught;" referring to the shoals of that fish which formerly made their way up the Hudson and through Fish Creek into Saratoga Lake.

The writings of the early French explorers in the " Jesuit Relations" seem to point definitely to the latter interpretation in preference to the former. The whole question, however, is so obscure as to make it scarcely worth consideration, except as a matter of curious speculation, for the employment of the idle hours of some *ennuied* visitor, or for the mystification of the nascent intellects of some youthful debating club. Should the Jesuit interpretation be the true one, it would seem that the dignity of godfather belongs to the lake in its relation to the village, instead of, as it is generally supposed, to the village in respect to the lake.

HOTELS.

From the time when the old pioneer, Gideon Putnam, built the first seventy feet of the present Union Hotel in the year 1802, Saratoga has been amply furnished with accommodations for man and beast. The late Congress Hall, which stood opposite Putnam's "Great House," almost rivalling it in extent, was commenced in 1811 ; also under the direction of the worthy founder of the village. It was opened to the public in 1815, and was destroyed by fire in 1866. The third of the grand hotels of Saratoga, the late United States, was commenced by John Ford in 1823, and extended in 1825. It afterwards passed into the hands of Marvin & Co., under whose management it gained the reputation of being one of the most excellent and most fashionable, as it was one of the most capacious establishments of the kind in the country. It was unfortunately burned to the ground in the summer of 1864.

This trio of grand hotels, the *Union*, the *Congress*, and the *United States*, became famous all the country through, and for many years continued to divide between them the patronage of the ever-increasing throngs of visitors to the Springs, and year by year they added new laurels to the reputation of the village as a place of convenient and pleasant resort.

Many other smaller, though scarcely less excellent establishments have grown up, from time to time, and have been well sustained, in the manner and degree of their respective characters and capacities.

Since the destruction of the old buildings of the *United*

States Hotel, and more recently of the *Congress* and the
Columbian, the public accommodations of Saratoga, though
still sufficient on a pinch, are of course not so ample as
they were, and as they soon will be again.

PIAZZA SCENE AT UNION HOTEL.

For the present the traveller may make himself at home
in the almost limitless halls of the *Union*, or within the

Union Hotel.

narrower, yet still ample boundaries of other hostelries, which will be introduced to his notice in the following glance at the various establishments.

UNION HOTEL.

Union Hotel, at present the largest and most fashionable hotel in the land, was the first considerable house of the kind erected in the village. It was commenced in the year 1802, while the place was still only a wild forest region, by Gideon Putnam, one of the earliest settlers and founders. At this time the edifice was about seventy feet in length. It has at different periods been rebuilt and enlarged, until it now covers, with its buildings, cottages, and courts, the broad area of seven acres. The main edifices have a front of five hundred and fifty feet and a depth of seven hundred feet, with almost a mile of colonnade and piazza. The entire accommodation of the place is sufficient for the comfort of fifteen hundred guests. The noble dining-hall of the Union, which has been added by the present proprietors, is probably the largest in the United States. It is two hundred and fifty feet long, fifty-three feet wide, and twenty feet high, and will comfortably seat twelve hundred people.

The Union came under the management of Major W. W. Leland, of the Metropolitan Hotel in New York, in the summer of 1864, when the close of the war released him from his duties as chief commissary of the Army of the Tennessee. With his characteristic enterprise, the new host set vigorously to work to enlarge and improve the premises, which he has done and is still doing in such a manner that there will soon be nothing left to do; and the gallant Major, like his predecessor, Alexander, may perchance yet be found weeping on the piazza of his hotel, because he can find no more difficulties to overcome. Even now the wide domain of the hotel is too limited in sphere for his expansive heart and genius, and, like his prototype, old Gideon Putnam, he is making the village itself the scene of his far-seeing enterprise and energy, and among other public works, has bestowed upon the place an opera-house, which in extent and appointments is not unworthy of a metropolitan location. Just now, too, he is pushing forward that excellent work, the new "Broad Avenue," from the springs to the lake, which, when completed, will be one of the most inviting drives in the world. May he long live to devise and execute many other schemes for the pleasure and glory of the place.

THE OLD AND NEW CONGRESS HALL.

This spacious edifice was commenced by Gideon Putnam, in the year 1811. In 1814 the property was purchased by Grandus Van Schoonhoven, who completed the buildings the following year, in accordance with the designs of Mr. Putnam.

Mr. Van Schoonhoven conducted the establishment until 1822, at which time he was joined by his nephew, Samuel H. Drake, and in 1823 by other partners. From 1823 to 1855 the house was leased from time to time to different parties, after which it fell under the administration of Messrs. Hawthorne & Hall. These gentlemen extended and greatly improved the property. They added a brick

The Old Congress Hall.

wing, which at its eastern end was six stories high, and extended from the older portion on the south side of Bath Street to Putnam Street. Many of the rooms also were at this time improved, and the whole house was refurnished in modern style. In 1857 Richard McMichael succeeded Mr. Hall in the firm, when further important additions were made. The house extended three hundred and seventy-nine feet on Broadway, and east on Bath Street to the west line of Putnam Street. The location is one of the most eligible and most convenient in the village, being in immediate proximity to the Congress Spring and its beautiful Park. The entire edifice was burnt to the ground in the summer of 1866.

The new and yet more extensive structure which is to take the place of the old building, and which is to be in part completed for the season of 1867, is of brick, with a façade of four hundred feet.

THE CLARENDON HOTEL.

The Clarendon is most agreeably situated on Broadway, embowered in a shady grove. Its outward presentment is very agreeable, while its inward appointments fulfil all the requirements of a first-class house. It ranks in all respects, except in size and the prestige of age and long service, with the Union and the Congress. It will accommodate some four hundred guests, perhaps. It possesses the considerable advantage of including within its grounds the popular fountain known as the Washington Spring.

3

TEMPLE GROVE HOTEL.

This excellent house, on Lincoln Avenue, stands in the shade of a fine maple and oak grove, upon an elevated site, which agreeably overlooks the village and its vicinage. It is a pleasant place, especially for families making a long sojourn at the Springs, and liking a quieter life than is to be found in the larger and more crowded houses.

In the winter season Temple Grove is favorably known as a Young Ladies' Seminary, under the charge of the Rev. Dr. Beecher.

THE AMERICAN HOTEL.

This house stands upon Broadway, between the Union and the old United States hotels. It has been much improved of late years, and is growing in the popular favor. It is one of the few of the large Saratoga hotels which are kept open all the year round. The charges, we believe, are less at the American than at the more fashionable resorts.

THE MARVIN HOUSE.

The Marvin affords excellent quarters for some two hundred and fifty guests. It is most eligibly located, and possesses all the needful comforts of a first-class house.

THE COLUMBIAN HOTEL.

This well-known house was unfortunately destroyed by fire in the summer of 1866. Its old guests, returning in

Saratoga Water-Cure.

1867, will be well pleased to find it rebuilt in better style even than before. The Columbian is conveniently situated a little way up Broadway.

THE WATER CURES.

The water-cure establishments of Dr. Bedrotha and of Dr. Hamilton are side by side on Congress Street and Broadway, directly opposite the Union Hotel. They are both excellent houses of their kind, and are always well filled. We scarcely need to commend them to invalids visiting the Springs.

THE OLD UNITED STATES HOTEL.

The late United States Hotel was a spacious and famous establishment. The various buildings were covered with a mile and a half of roofing, and with the grounds and courts occupied the generous area of six acres. The house was built in part in 1823, by John Ford. It passed afterwards into the hands of James M. Marvin & Co., by whom it was successfully conducted, until the time of its destruction by fire in 1864.

There were guests of the *United States* who had summered under its hospitable roofs year after year, from youth to age, storing up thousands of happy memories of the old place, which were rudely disturbed when it passed away. It is appetizing even to think of the luxurious dinners and the dainty suppers which were spread for so many years upon its generous tables; and the gouty foot becomes the light fantastic toe again, at the remembrance of all the gay revelry it once shared in the old festive halls. Endless and varied are the associations which cling to the spot, and both happy and sad the memories it will awaken. Many staid matrons and grave sires, now thousands of miles away, who whilom danced and sighed together in the vanished parlors and the silent groves, will recall scenes of great pith and moment, which perchance gave color—rosy color, let us hope—to all their after-life.

THE SARATOGA HOP.

Music and dancing are of course very important items in the catalogue of Saratoga occupations, as they are at all spas and places of summer recreation; and the appointments at our Springs, in this wise, are most ample and excellent. In former days, the watering-place "institution" known as the Hop was a rarer and more serious affair, in the preparation, than it is in our improved age. Long intervals separated the happy occasions, and all sorts of preparatory labor was required. The dining-halls had to be vacated for the nonce, so that the apartments could be seasonably converted into ball-rooms: thus the dinner of the day became a hurried affair, and "tea" had to be snatched as best it might. Now each of the principal hotels has its especial altar to Terpsichore, and the lamp of incense is forever trimmed and burning. The guest dines and sups at ease and leisure, and when the diurnal

The Late United States Hotel.

hour arrives for the saltatory devotions of the evening, he or she steals a glance at the approving mirror, calls the conquering smile to the lips, points the expectant toe with required grace, and floats at once into the elysian maze.

The " Hop," when it reaches the proportions and dignity of a ball, is an occasional and more elaborate mystery, and is held at one particular " house," in behalf of the whole : the toilette becomes a matter of life and death, to the utter forgetfulness of the price of gold and " universal suffrage." The order of the dancing, and the programme of the orchestra are solemnly considered and formally announced ; and last, though not least, agreeable refreshments are provided for the sustenance of the exhausted devotees. On these signal occasions, the whole village population, both exotic and native, unite in joyous revelry.

It is not, however, on occasions only, frequent as they may be, that Saratoga dances. On the contrary, it is forever dancing or drinking—the one exercise being the omega as the other is the alpha of its butterfly life. Each and every night bands of skilled musicians discourse at the hotels, and those who will may waltz and polk unceasingly.

A peep at these gay and brilliant scenes, and at the beaux and belles, in all their gorgeous array of trailing robes and gleaming jewels, will explain to the wondering novice the meaning and use of the travelling arks, known at the present time as " Saratoga trunks." One has but to watch for a single day the successive toilettes, as they change from morn to noon, from noon to eve, and from eve to night—to see that the massive structures are, comparatively

3*

speaking, and considering what they are required to hold—nothing but carpet-bags after all.

It is just possible that the packing of these little bags, with their little stores, may have cost some painful privations and some pitiful pinching around the fireside at home; or it may be followed, anon, by the lost credit and the broken heart of some over-indulgent pater-familias, delving in his Wall Street lair; but what of that! we have had a merry and a jolly time, our little vanity and our petty pride have been gratified to the full—we have happily excited each other's envy—perchance his hate—and have picked up mutual impressions, good or bad, as wide of the truth as is desirable for people who may possibly become intimately associated in after-life.

Should any such idle reflections as these flit across the minds of the fair wives and daughters and sisters and *fiancées*, as they seek their late repose, they will doubtless find a sufficiently soothing balm when they awake, and picking up the morning paper, read Jenkins' brilliant description of their triumphs of the night before;—as how, for example, the lovely Mrs. Col. D—h—y, of New York, wore a white tarleton double skirt; the under skirt elaborately trimmed with ruchings of green and white tarleton; the corsage of white silk, cut low and pointed, and headed with green leaves, with berthe and sleeves of white tarleton, puffed and trimmed with green ruchings, to correspond with skirt; glove of delicate light green, hair *creped*, head light and waterfall heavy, with clusters of pearls and diamonds.

Or how the charming Miss B—r—y, of Philadelphia, was deliciously robed in a white organdie, with deep flounce, with puffings of the same, lined with pink ribbons, corsage *décolette*, and berthe with tucks and insertings : sleeves long and full : a wreath of pink and white roses, dropping from the right shoulder, diagonally to the head of the flounce in the skirt. Hair powdered with diamond dust, and waterfall of *négligé* curls.

Jenkins will be gracious and pardon us, we trust, if our text fails, as is likely, to do justice to his amiable and facile pen.

THE LELAND OPERA HOUSE.

For those who cannot exist in the country without all the luxurious adjuncts of city life, Saratoga has built its Opera House, where may be witnessed, from time to time, as the " stars " may happen to shine on the village, the mysteries of the Thespian art and the strains of the lyric stage.

Though not pretending to rival La Scala or the Grand Opera, the Saratoga house nevertheless makes excellent attraction in opera and concert—sometimes offering the best talent and genius of the time. Of course neither visitors nor residents neglect to avail themselves of all the opportunities it affords. The building is also very useful for the various miscellaneous entertainments which fortune may provide, and for such impromptu festivals—fairs, *tableaux*, and the like—which the wit and genius of the visitors may suggest.

The Opera House is one of the many great debts which the people and guests of Saratoga owe to the large and liberal enterprise of Major Leland, the popular host of the "Union." It is the property of the Messrs. Leland, by whom it was devised and built, at a cost of some eighty thousand dollars.

The house stands a little way south of the rear of the Union Hotel. It is imposing in its exterior, and has every possible convenience and comfort within, with accommodation for an audience of fifteen hundred or more people. It is surrounded, indeed almost buried, by colonnade and piazza, which afford delightful breathing-room on sultry summer nights.

The Opera House was appropriately inaugurated on the night of the Fourth of July, 1865, with the grand ball, which followed the memorable dinner given on that day by Major Leland, of the Union Hotel, to his *confrères* of the Army of the Tennessee; at which a larger number of illustrious generals, majors, colonels, captains, and officers of all ranks assisted, than ever met before on any field.

At another time the house was used for the successful exhibition of *tableaux vivants*, which was given by the guests of the "Union" in aid of the sufferers by the fatal Portland fire. This latter occasion, no less than the opening ball, will be long pleasantly remembered in connection with the new Opera House. The net proceeds of the tableaux entertainment reached the generous sum of nearly two thousand dollars, Major Leland contributing the use of the building, and Mr. Kent, one of the guests, defraying the other expenses.

THE MINERAL WATERS.

The valley stretch, which is more or less occupied by the Saratoga waters, is of very considerable extent, reaching from the banks of the Hudson,—even as far south as the city of Albany—to a distance of about sixty miles, to Argyle, in Washington County; the general course being, from the most southerly point, northwest, via Ballston, to the village of Saratoga, and thence northeastward. The waters are of course most abundant at the particular locality from which they are named—and in a business sense may be said to exist there alone.

The springs issue from the limestone strata, which everywhere underlies the sandy loam upon which the village is built, most of them showing themselves along the banks of the little brook which traverses the place.

The medicinal virtues of the Saratoga waters are of a rare and very varied character, efficacious in the treatment of many troublesome complaints, and invaluable to the partial invalid and all generally dilapidated and used-up visitors, as a pleasant and sure cathartic and tonic. Taken in reasonable quantity, and particularly in connection with the fresh air, exercise, physical and mental repose, and the pleasurable recreations incident to the routine of Saratoga life, the waters never fail to provoke appetite, promote digestion, exorcise the blues and the bile, and to generally purify, strengthen, and cheer both body and mind. For a detailed and scientific account of their properties and virtues in relation to the various classes and stages of disease, in the cure and correction of which they may be used, the suffering reader is referred to the excellent Handbook of Dr. R. L. Allen, a distinguished resident physician.

Of course the waters are employed chiefly in the summer season, but they are said to be equally beneficial when taken during the coldest winter months. Change of season does not appear to affect their temperature, specific gravity, or chemical composition ; and they lie too deeply imbedded in the bosom of old mother earth to be at all vexed by the fresh waters on the surface or by the spring or autumn rains.

Besides the immense quantities daily consumed by visitors at the fountains, large supplies of some of the waters are bottled and exported, for home use, to all parts of the country ; so much so indeed that they are to be found among the specifics of every considerable drug-store in the land.

The whole category of the Saratoga waters embraces a list altogether too extended for individual mention ; but there are some dozen or more, distinguished from the crowd, and possessing general fame and favor, of which it will be proper to speak in some detail in our chapter upon the mineral waters, of which the few pages just written are meant to serve as preface.

Among these stars in the liquid firmament are the Congress, the most popularly known of all the group, the Empire, the High Rock, the Columbian, the Hamilton, the Putnam, the Pavilion, and the Star or Iodine, as it was formerly named.

Congress Spring.

CONGRESS SPRING.

Congress Spring, the most famous and most fashionable of the Saratoga waters, was discovered in 1792, just seventy-five years after the visit of Sir William Johnson to the High Rock.

A hunting-party happened to observe numerous deer-tracks, leading in a particular direction ; and, following the trail with some curiosity, to see whither it led, they stumbled upon a new mineral spring, which the deer, it appears, were in the habit of visiting in their search for salt. The water issued from a rock about three feet in height, through an aperture midway between the top and the ground. Among the Nimrods was a member of Congress named Gilman, and in honor of this gentleman and his high position, the new fountain was christened Congress Spring.

The water was at first secured by pressing a cup against the rock, through which means not more than one quart per minute was obtained. To increase the yield, and to economize the loss by this primitive mode of drawing, Gideon Putnam, who was at all times wide awake, set about clearing and tubing the spring. He first turned the brook some few feet from its original course, and, guided by the bubbles of gas, which rose from the channel of the stream, he sunk a shaft into the rock. The water thereupon ceased to issue from the old aperture, but rose in ample supply from the new opening, and was at once secured as completely as was practicable, by means of a tube made of pine planks. Putnam, we are told, had, at one time, two potash kettles employed in evaporating the water and precipitating salts, which he put up in small packages, and sold, to the amount, sometimes, of several hundred dollars a year. The speculation, however, soon ceased to be profitable, when it was found that the salts, redissolved, did not produce Congress water.

The property upon which the Congress Spring is situated was purchased in the year 1826, by Mr. John Clarke, a gentlemen of culture and enterprise, and who had had considerable experience in the management of such matters. To him, indeed, belonged the honor—such as it was—of having opened the first soda fountain in New York.

The spring had risen gradually in reputation from the day of its discovery, and when it fell under the control of Mr. Clarke, it had acquired a wide-spread fame, which his administration did not fail to heighten and extend. He very soon began to bottle the water for exportation, and with so much success as to realize from that source alone a very handsome income.

Mr. Clarke added to his possessions in the vicinity from time to time, and to such an extent that, when he died, in 1846, he was the owner of no less than one thousand acres of land in the neighborhood of his spring. That he was a man of fine taste and of liberal views, is evident from the admirable improvements which he made all around, as in the decoration of the fountain, and more particularly in the charming park which lies south and east of the spring, and which his enterprise conjured from the slimy swamp.

The water of Congress Spring is an excellent cathartic, very agreeable to the palate, and most cheering to the spirits. It is employed with good result in almost all cases of weak digestion, of dyspepsia, and of general debility.

Crowds gather around the pretty fountain in the early summer mornings to win appetite for breakfast, and life for the pleasures of the day. Old or young, sick or well, everybody drinks; for the Congress fountain is the morning exchange to which all resort, even as the ball-room is the gathering-place at night. It is a gay group, that, which the rising sun always looks down upon by the Congress fountain, and as pleasant to see as any of many bright *tableaux vivants* to be found at Saratoga.

The Congress water, by recent analysis, is found to be composed as follows:

To one Gallon.

	GRAINS.
Chloride of Sodium, ...	360.560
Carbonate of Soda, ...	8.000
Carbonate of Lime, ...	82.321
Carbonate of Magnesia, ...	78.242
Carbonate of Iron, ...	3.645
Iodide of Soda, ...	4.531
Silica, ...	0.510
Alumina	0.231
Solid contents, ...	538.040
Carbonic Acid, ...	340.231
Atmospheric Air, ...	4.000
Gaseous contents, . . .	344.231

THE HIGH ROCK SPRING.

This curiously formed fountain is the oldest of the great and numerous Saratoga family of waters, being the veritable

4

spring at which the first white visitor to the region—Sir William Johnson—drank, just one hundred years ago.

HIGH ROCK SPRING.

The High Rock Spring is unusually interesting, both from its medicinal virtues and for its singular geological structure.

The rock from whence the spring issues is a conical deposit of limestone, three feet and a half high and twenty-four and one-third feet in circumference. On the top there is an aperture, of cylindrical form and a foot in diameter. Recent bold excavations, under the direction of its present proprietors, show that their singular formation, which has for so many years been a subject of speculation and mystery, extends only a few inches below the surface, and may be easily moved. Upon displacing it, it was found to contain a chamber about two feet in diameter, and below it there was a reservoir filled with the bubbling water to the depth of ten feet. Hidden in this unveiled reservoir, there were found numerous tumblers, which had been accidentally dropped, from time to time, through the aperture. The soil in all directions was incrusted with the deposits from the water; but directly beneath the rock there was found, strange to relate, the trunk of a tree, a foot and a half in diameter, and of sufficient solidity to admit of its being sawed in pieces and removed. This tree unquestionably fell, on the spot where it lay, before the time when the formation of the rock above it commenced—that is to say, about three thousand years ago !

Still a few feet below this most venerable dead man of the woods, there was also found the body of an oak of about eight inches in diameter, and but slightly decayed.

When the excavations, by means of which these singular facts were brought to light, had reached to the depth of twelve feet, it became evident that further digging would expose the crevice in the solid rock, from which the fountain flows, and bolder venture was foreborne.

The High Rock, thus displaced, is to be again set over the fountain, when it is expected that it will be overflown by the water, as it has been through so many centuries gone by. The rock has been formed by the mineral substances which are held in solution in the springs, as magnesia, lime, and iron, intermixed with the leaves and twigs of trees, and other particles.

The highly-charged water of this spring, upon rising to

the air, can hold but one volume of the gas in solution, and has therefore precipitated its excess of carbonates, particle by particle, around the aperture of the fountain, until the accumulation and the uniting of these precipitates has, in the lapse of time, formed the great mass of calcareous tufa so long known as the High Rock.

Other formations of the kind are to be seen at Saratoga, in a greater or less extent. The Flat Rock displays similar deposits, and at the mouth of the Empire Spring there was found an accumulation of tufa about the size of an inverted two-quart bowl. Similar deposits are indeed always being made under like conditions; but they rarely remain so undisturbed, by currents of water or other agencies, as to obtain any very great bulk, and never the extraordinary dimensions of the High Rock, which is supposed to be the largest and most wonderful specimen of the kind in the world.

Dr. Valentine Seaman, in his description, in 1809, of this celebrated spring and its magnificent tufa, says: "The more we reflect upon it, the more we must be convinced of the important place this rock ought to hold among the wonderful works in nature. Had it stood on the borders of the Lago D'Agnans, the noted Grotto del Cani (which, since the peculiar properties of carbonic acid have been known, burden almost every book which treats of the gas), would never have been heard of beyond the environs of Naples; while this fountain, in its place, would have been deservedly celebrated in story and spread upon canvas, to the admiration of the world, as one of its greatest curiosities."

The High Rock Spring is situated in the more northern

part of the village, but a short distance from the Empire
and the Star or Iodine springs. In the rear of the springs
the rocks rise to the height of thirty to forty feet, affording
opportunity for more picturesque embellishments than the
spot yet displays. The water of the High Rock is abundant and of very uniform quality. It is an admirable tonic,
and of greater force as a stimulant than the more frequented
Congress fountain by which it has been, in a great measure, supplanted in the popular esteem.

Dr. Allen's latest tests of this spring show the following
component parts:

To one Gallon.

	GRAINS.
Chloride of Sodium, ...	190.223
Carbonate of Magnesia, ...	62.100
Carbonate of Lime, ...	71.533
Carbonate of Soda, ...	18.421
Carbonate of Iron, ...	4.233
Iodide of Soda, ...	2.177
Silex and Alumina, ...	2.500
Hydriobromate of Potash—a small quantity.	
Solid contents, . . .	351.197

THE EMPIRE SPRING.

The Empire, the most northerly of the series of springs,
lies beyond the High Rock, at the head of and to the right
of Broadway. Next to the Congress, it is the most fashionable fountain in the village, although it did not come into
notice until the year 1846. Directly behind the spring
there lies a bluff of Mohawk limestone, about forty feet in

4*

height, resting on a ledge of calciferous sandstone. The water issued through a perforation in this sandstone, which circumstance greatly facilitated the securing of it, with its full complement of gas, by allowing a tube to be scribed to the surface of the rock.

The column of water in the tube above the rock is nine and a half feet—the tube itself being eleven and a half feet. The fountain yields the liberal supply of seventy-five gallons per hour. Despite its remote position, it has already, in the comparatively short time in which it has been in use, acquired a high reputation, and is attended daily by large numbers of visitors.

It is considered to be an excellent cathartic and alterative water, and is serviceable in a very wide range of cases.

The component parts of the Empire Spring, as seen in the analysis of one gallon of the water, are given as follows:

To one Gallon.

	GRAINS.
Chloride of Sodium, ...	270.000
Carbonate of Lime, ...	145.321
Carbonate of Magnesia, ...	43.123
Carbonate of Soda, ...	30.304
Carbonate of Iron, ...	3.000
Iodide of Soda, ...	8.000
Silica, ...	1.000

Solid contents, . . .	500.748
Gaseous contents, . . .	700
Specific gravity, ...	1.0056

COLUMBIAN SPRING.

This pleasant water, with its pretty protecting dome, is familiar enough to all visitors to Saratoga,—standing as it does in such close proximity to the Congress Spring, in full

COLUMBIAN SPRING.

view from the piazza of the Union Hotel. It is one of the oldest of the mineral springs, having been opened by Gideon Putnam asearly as 1806.

The water of the Columbian is ferruginous, and contains:

a great quantity of carbonic acid in a free state, which, bubbling to the surface, gives it the appearance of a boiling spring.

The general properties of this water are very much the same as those of its neighbor, the Congress, though varying in their relative qualities. It is a very strong tonic, and, in consequence, should be used with caution, and not too freely.

The following ingredients are found in an analysis of one gallon of the Columbian fountain :

	GRAINS.
Chloride of Sodium, ...	290.501
Carbonate of Soda, ...	26.000
Carbonate of Magnesia, ...	40.321
Carbonate of Lime, ...	90.000
Carbonate of Iron, ...	6.000
Iodide of Soda, ...	3.000
Silica and Alumina, ...	1.531
Solid contents, . . .	457.353
Carbonic Acid, . . .	330.000

THE WASHINGTON SPRING.

The Washington, otherwise known as White's Spring, lies about six hundred feet southeast of the Congress fountain, in the grounds of the Clarendon Hotel. It is the only spring of all the group which is situated on this, the west side of Broadway. It was opened as early as 1806, by old Gideon Putnam, but remained unused until 1858, when

Mr. John H. White, into whose hands the property had passed two years before, undertook to restore it, by tracing the water to the place of its escape from the rock. The undertaking proved to be both toilsome and hazardous.

A shaft, eleven feet square and thirty feet long, was sunk, but no water rose through it. The explorations were then continued a distance of thirty feet, by means of a substantial tunnel. During the operations, the earth gave way, when the water and gas poured in with such velocity, as to leave the laborers barely time to escape with their lives. No less than twelve thousand gallons of water, and twice as much carbonic acid gas, entered the shaft in the brief space of fifteen minutes.

After a while another shaft was sunk, and the earth broke through a second time, again endangering the lives of the workmen. The third attempt, which was made at another point, proved more successful. The shaft used at this time was twenty feet in diameter, and was constructed in a very massive and substantial manner. When it was completed the explorers had the satisfaction of seeing their oft-renewed efforts amply repaid. The water rose sparkling and bright through the tube, and has ever since continued to flow over the top in free and full supply.

The fountain is highly esteemed, and is much resorted to. The water is of a very lively character, and is serviceable in a great variety of ways.

THE PAVILION SPRING.

The Pavilion lies a few feet east of the pleasant promenade called the Willow Walk, in the rear of the Columbian

Hotel. A few rods southeast of the Pavilion is the Flat Rock Spring; and the Empire, High Rock, and Star fountains are not far above.

This spring was discovered at an early day, but was not utilized until the year 1839, when it was tubed, with much cost and labor, by Daniel McLaren, the owner of the property at that period.

It lay in the midst of a deep morass, from which it rose through an alluvial deposit of forty feet in depth. Under Mr. McLaren's efforts, and afterwards through the enterprise of the Messrs. Walton, into whose possession the grounds again fell, the morass was cleared, and otherwise greatly improved. The channel of the brook was turned, pleasant walks were made, and shade-trees were planted, so that the spot is at this time an agreeable place of resort.

The analysis of the Pavilion shows the following properties:

To one Gallon.

	GRAINS.
Chloride of Sodium, ...	183.816
Carbonate of Soda, ...	6.000
Carbonate of Lime, ...	59.593
Carbonate of Magnesia, ...	58.266
Carbonate of Iron, ...	4.133
Iodide of Soda and Bromine of Potassa, . . .	2.566
Silex and Alumina, ...	1.000
Solid contents, . .	315.372
Gaseous contents, . .	372.499

THE HAMILTON SPRING.

The Hamilton Spring is another of the many which were discovered and tubed by Gideon Putnam, in the early part of the present century. It is situated a few rods northeast of Congress Spring, and in the rear of the late Congress Hall. It was retubed and placed in its present condition by the late Dr. Clarke, to whom the village and the public at large are so much indebted for improvements, not only in the development of the mineral resources of the valley, but for contributions to the growth and beauty of the town in many valuable ways. The water rises in the tube almost to the level of the ground, bubbling up by means of the rapid escape of fixed air, not unlike a boiling spring. During the past thirty or forty years it has been employed satisfactorily as an alterative. It is beneficial also as a cathartic, in cases of very weak stomachs, where rude, active waters—as those, for example, of the Congress Spring —might be too active and exhausting.

The following is the analysis of this spring, as made by Dr. Allen

To one Gallon.

	GRAINS.
Chloride of Sodium, ...	298.656
Carbonate of Soda, ...	34.250
Carbonate of Lime, ...	97.996
Carbonate of Magnesia, ...	39.066
Carbonate of Iron, ...	4.625

	GRAINS.
Iodide of Soda, .	3.598
Silex and Alumina, .	1.000

Solid contents, .	479.191
Carbonic Acid, .	320.777
Atmospheric Air, .	1.461

Gaseous contents, .	322.238

Temperature, 48°

THE PUTNAM SPRING.

The Putnam Spring is but a few steps to the northeast of the Hamilton, and midway between Broadway and Putnam streets. It was tubed and brought into use in the year 1835, by Mr. Lewis Putnam. Since that time it has been retubed and improved in various ways. The water has been bottled, and is freely used by visitors with very satisfactory results. It contains more iron among its ingredients than any of the mineral waters of the neighborhood, —excepting, perhaps, the Columbian. The taste is by no means unpleasant. Attached to this spring is an excellent bathing-house, in which the mineral water is used. There are, also, well-ordered bathing facilities at the Hamilton Spring, last referred to in our catalogue. Many visitors find as much benefit from the use of the Saratoga waters in this way as in taking them internally. The external application, indeed, while at all times a very pleasurable and exhilarating remedy, is much less likely to produce injurious effects through excessive use, than is the drinking of the waters as indulged in by many visitors.

ANALYSIS OF THE PUTNAM SPRING.

To one Gallon.

	GRAINS.
Chloride of Sodium, ...	220.000
Carbonate of Soda, ...	15.321
Carbonate of Magnesia, ...	45.500
Carbonate of Lime, ...	70.433
Carbonate of Iron, ...	5.333
Iodide of Soda, ...	2.500
Silex and Alumina, ...	1.500

	Solid contents, . .	300.587

Carbonic Acid, ...	317.753
Atmospheric Air, ...	3.080

	Gaseous contents, . .	320.833

Temperature, 48°

THE STAR SPRING.

The Star Spring was at one time known as the President, and yet more recently as the Iodine. It is situated in the upper part of the village, not far from the High Rock. It has been analyzed by Dr. Allen, with the following results :

To one Gallon.

	GRAINS.
Chloride of Sodium, ...	180.731
Carbonate of Soda, ...	3.000

Carbonate of Magnesia, ... 30.000
Carbonate of Lime, ... 74.213
Carbonate of Iron, ... 1.000
Iodide of Sodium, ... 3.235
Silica and Alumina, ...500

Solid contents, . . . 292.697

Carbonic Acid and Atmospheric Air, . . 335.000

STAR SPRING.

THE EXCELSIOR SPRING.

The Excelsior is a name recently bestowed upon one of the group of mineral fountains known as the Ten Springs. It flows directly from the primeval rock, and is of great purity and excellence. It possesses, like its numerous sister waters, strong diuretic, alterative, and tonic virtues. The latest analysis shows the Excelsior to be composed as follows :

	GRAINS.
Chloride of Sodium, ...	375.8996
Carbonate of Lime, ...	76.0160
Carbonate of Magnesia, ...	30.4437
Carbonate of Soda, ...	10.3520
Silicate of Potassa, ...	6.9827
Silicate of Soda, ...	3.7672
Carbonate of Iron, ...	2.8086
Sulphate of Soda, ...	1.5503
Solid contents in one gallon, . . .	507.8203

THE " A " SPRING.

This fountain is situated some twenty rods above the " Empire." It was opened in 1866, and promises to become a very popular resort.

THE TEN SPRINGS.

The Ten Springs are grouped within the circumference of an acre of ground, about a mile northeast of the village, and may be reached either by a carriage-road or by a pleasant winding path through the woods. They were discovered in the year 1814.

THE ELLIS SPRING.

This fountain springs from the side of a deep ravine about two miles south of the village. A densely wooded brook traverses the gorge, and presents some picturesque features worth seeing. The water here is an agreeable beverage, and if situated otherwise than amidst such a wealth of waters as this region offers, would be of great value.

REED'S SPRING.

This fountain may be mentioned in our *resumé* of the Saratoga waters, though it is not included in the village group. It lies, indeed, far away in South Argyle, in Washington County, the northern terminus of the great mineral valley. It is an acidulous carbonated water, and escapes through a fissure in a stratum of Mohawk limestone. It is not a very sparkling water, but is at least harmless, and, with its slightly acidulated taste, is by no means disagreeable to the palate.

It is sometimes used as a yeast, in the concoction of the diet known in the vicinity as " spring-water rolls."

THE WHITE SULPHUR SPRING.

This fountain is situated on the east side of Saratoga Lake, in a little picturesque ravine about a mile and a half below Snake Hill. Not far from the lake, a distance say of twenty rods, the visitor will see a niche in the south bank of the small brook which runs through the ravine just mentioned, and in the heart of this niche, at the base of the bluff, he will find the spring. The water is heavily impregnated with sulphurated hydrogen gas, and is not to be commended as an agreeable drink, whatever may be its sanitary merits.

The water boils up in a basin some eight feet wide by two feet in depth. It is so remarkably clear, that it is said a needle's eye may be distinctly seen at the bottom of the fountain. The gas bubbles up from among the pebbles and sand in a very lively style, inviting the unwary to drink and be—very little pleased with the flavor of the dose.

At one time a hotel and bathing-house offered acceptable accommodations at this spring, but like so many of the Saratoga hotels, they were unluckily burned one day.

The grove and greensward in which the spring is centred is a pretty place, and is much affected by the village picnic parties.

THE INDIAN ENCAMPMENT.

Not the least interesting of the regular pastimes of Saratoga is a visit to the Indian Encampment, to be seen on the skirts of the village every year, as the summer days come round. These red-men visit the place, not as they follow the war-path, nor in quest of game, nor even to drink of the waters and be healed, as did their forefathers sometimes in ages gone by; but simply with an eye to business, like the fashionable modiste, whose gorgeous sign appears in Broadway every season about the same time.

They are not to be mistaken for the Massasoits, the Philips, the Canonicuses, the Black Hawks, and the Tecumsehs of the old warrior age of aboriginal story—nor for the interesting gentry of that stripe who figure in poetry and fiction: on the contrary, they are of a very opposite and degenerate class, being simply a gipsey band—half or quarter breeds, of Canadian French and negro blood, with plenty

5*

of the vicious reality and but little of the beautiful romance of the conventional Indian character.

Their encampment, notwithstanding, affords scenes and incidents most agreeable to the eye, and themes of thought quite worth considering. The white tents, gleaming amongst the forest verdure, and the bright costumes and varied action of the changing groups, make pleasant pictures to frame in one's memory of the place. And there is much to see and study in the variety of their manufacture and merchandise; their gorgeously decorated bows and quivers—harmless enough now, alas!—the pretty bead-work of the squaws—the papooses oscillating in their rustic cradles, and many rare curiosities, for use or ornament, and peculiar to Indian life. If generously disposed, the visitor may set up pennies for targets, and as prizes for the little red *garçons* when they bring them down, as they are sure to do with their flying arrows. In the evening hours the light of the camp-fires lends a new and yet brighter charm to the scene.

THE RAILWAY STATION.

The stage-office, the steamboat-landing, or the railway-station, as the case may be, is always a point of interest to visitors at a watering-place. In the busy city, people may come and go by thousands, but who ever thinks of the arrivals or the departures, unless, perchance, he have a friend now and then to welcome in or to speed away? Who, indeed, will even stop to shake hands, much less to cross the street, to greet an acquaintance unseen for months, and who may, for aught that is known, have shivered at the poles or roasted on the equator within the interval? It is not thus at the lazy summer retreats. Here there is time enough for more than mere civility. Here the hard, pre-occupied business air, the devil-take-the-hindmost expression of selfish absorption, is exchanged for the ready recognition, the cordial greeting, and an amiability and even an affection-ateness of welcome worthy of the heart of a " Cherryble " brother. With leisure enough for friendly curiosity and for active sympathy (if the heart is by nature large enough for the high humanities), people at Saratoga, as at all sum-mer lounges, are interested in the incomings and outgoings of their fellow-men ; and, as the best means of gratifying this laudable feeling, and perchance of killing a dull hour at the same time, they are daily *habituées* of the railway-station, at such times as the ups and downs may be falling due,—watching with more or less eagerness if perchance some friend may turn up, and saluting even a slight city acquaintance with a warmth undreamed of in the colder social temperature of the town. There is nothing like such pleasant leisure and grateful rest to thaw the frozen heart.

At Saratoga the facilities for such greetings and fare-wells are excellent, for the railway-station is a most agree-able spot, standing in a broad, open square, and within a brief walk of all the chief hotels.

BROADWAY.

Pity 'tis that the godfathers and godmothers of the chief street in " our village " did not bestow upon it a patronymic less suggestive of dust and dirt, of hurry and unrest, than are the frightful syllables, to country-loving ears, of " Broadway." Still, a rose with any other name, the poet tells us, will smell as sweet; and our Saratoga Broadway is unquestionably a noble avenue, miles in length, ample in breadth, and withal shaded, for the most part, with splendid elms. It has its crowds, to be sure, as has the Broadway below, on Manhattan Island; but they are crowds of holiday loungers —not hurrying bulls and bears; of gay-liveried equipages— not lumbering drays and omnibuses; and should you meet a friend, after a year or so's absence, you may, *en passant*, give him somewhat more than a hasty nod. Neither are we troubled here with noisy pavements, Russ, Belgian, or asphalte; and sad-eyed mendicants beset us not as we move along.

The entire length of this fine street is more than three miles in a direct line, and even in the more thronged portions the crowd is lost amidst the verdure of the double line of beautiful trees which traverses the whole promenade: or the varied hues of the gay attire, contrasted with and seen, here and there, amidst the green leafage, produces still a feeling of rural rather than of metropolitan life. Much of the street, also, is at all times quiet and country-looking enough, for the hotel and business quarters occupy only a comparatively small part, at the lower extremity. This quarter, as far as it extends, is gay enough, with the showy shops of the migratory modistes, the restaurants and saloons, and the other appendages of a fashionable watering-place, superadded to the local business of the village. To all this is to be added the throngs which lounge on the broad piazzas of the hotels, or which are coming and

going to and from the many fountains. Altogether our
Saratoga Broadway is a very pleasant sort of Broadway—
a clever *rus in urbe.*

THE PARK.

The beautiful crescent-shaped grounds around the Congress Spring were reclaimed from the deep and dank swamp
by Mr. John Clarke, the former owner of the property, who
purchased the farm, in which it was included, of the Living-
stons, in 1826.

This tract, once so dreary and doleful, is now one of the
chiefest landscape beauties of the village. The topography
of the grounds is very agreeably diversified, showing fine
reaches of meadow and lawn, and pretty hill-slopes, open
glade, and shady copse, all interspersed with little winding
walks or broader promenades. The sunny hours may be
charmingly spent in the bosky nooks of the Park, in the
quiet companionship of books, or in cosy gossip with some
of the many old friends always to be found at the Springs.
The Park presents a brilliant face on a bright summer
morning, when the throngs of tripping feet tend hither
from all points, to drink the sparkling waters of the famous
Congress or Columbian springs ; and when many an early
riser, bent upon enjoying " the free, the fresh, the early
morning air," takes his " constitutional " along its promenades. On soft summery moonlight nights, too, when the
gentle zephyrs bring grateful coolness to the heated brow,
what a delight it is to steal away from the glaring halls and
the torrid ball-rooms of the thronged hotels, and wander
up and down the wee hills and dales ! It is possible that

there may be gouty sires, or aged dowagers, or grim un-
social bachelors, who may think this sort of thing all bosh ;
but it won't do to say so to Damon and Chloe, as they glide
along the shadiest walks—the shadiest even in moonlight—
linked arm-in-arm, perchance hand-in-hand, drinking in
from eye and lip deep draughts, sweeter to the taste and
more stirring to the blood than all the carbonates of all the
springs from one end of the mineral valley to the other.

THE CHURCHES.

Saratoga, with all its fun and fashion and its material
enjoyments, is not without its share of serious life, any more
than are graver and duller places ; as the church-spires,
here and there, will testify.   No one, whatever may chance
to be his creed, need, from want of opportunity, neglect his
religious devotions in the rush of worldly delights ; since
the temple-doors are everywhere open to all sects and
denominations, Jew or Gentile, Catholic or Protestant,
High Church or Low Church, orthodox or heterodox, whatever he may be.

Some of the church edifices are elegant affairs ; quite
worthy of the oblation of the most refined city congrega-
tions, and ministered to by pastors of culture and repute.

The *Episcopal church*, on Washington Street, is a modern edifice of stone, most pleasing in its architecture, and
suitable in all its interior adornments.   A handsome contri-
bution to the exchequer of the society was made recently
through the medium of an amateur exhibition of *tableaux
vivants* on the stage of the Leland Opera House.

The *Presbyterian church* is a fine brick edifice, of ample dimensions, pleasantly located some little distance up Broadway. The site, we believe, was presented by Henry Walton, one of the early residents and benefactors of Saratoga. Mr. Walton was a gentleman of great taste and enterprise, which he displayed in various contributions to the progress and embellishment of the place. Among other good works, he created the beautiful estate known as " Woodlawn," and built the pleasant residence of " Pine Grove," occupied by the venerable Chancellor Walworth.

The *Baptist church* is on Washington Street, opposite the Episcopal church. The site was presented by the old pioneer Gideon Putnam, when he left the land to the first religious society which might be ready to occupy it.

The *Methodist church* is also conveniently located among the other places of worship on Washington Street.

The *Catholic church* occupies a commanding and most agreeable location upon Broadway, just above the Clarendon Hotel.

COUNTRY-SEATS.

The villa residences of Saratoga are numerous and attractive, though they do not make so marked a feature in the character of the place as at Newport. They may do so, however, by-and-by, as the high virtues of the climate come to be better appreciated, and as the means and appliances of luxurious life increase. The neighborhood, certainly, offers great inducements for summer, if not permanent residence; with its unusual facilities for country seclusion, within call of all the gayeties of city life. The bracing, healthful atmosphere, the invaluable mineral waters, the varied social resources, the picturesque scenery, and the easy access, all combined, should certainly surround the Springs with a cordon of sumptuous villas and picturesque " boxes," unsurpassed by any locality in the land.

To some people it may be, sometimes, too much of a good thing to live always in the hurly-burly of the great hotels ; but then to these even, a quiet private home, apart from and yet within immediate reach of the great world, seems to promise the desired *juste milieu.*

It is not within the scope of our purpose here to make individual mention of the private homes of the village, but the visitor will not fail to see and enjoy them in his rides and walks through the neighborhood.

THE SARATOGA RACES.

Our village gives fair promise of soon becoming—even if it is not already—the head-centre of the sports of the turf in America. Its famous race-course, which lies one and a half mile out of town, and which was surveyed and laid out in 1863 by Charles H. Ballard, is the largest in the Union, not even excepting the great Fashion Course on Long Island, and the more modern Jerome Park in New York. It is a favorite resort of the leading "horse-men" of the land, and the best-blooded steeds are brought hither every season for the display of their prowess in wind and limb. The great equine contests come off in July or August, when all the region runs mad with excitement, scarcely less infectious than that which may be seen at

Epsom, through the wild doings of a Derby-day. Everybody goes who has the good fortune to find a carriage or a cart, a cab or a cob to carry them, or who is able to traverse the short distance on that universal self-acting vehicle, vulgarly known as Shank's mare. The programme of exercises offers more than the usual variety to which the item of "running races" has been added within two or three years past. Of course it is a jolly occasion, and the interest, if not the betting, runs high. Such sports are always inspiriting, and at Saratoga they stir up the blood as effectually as the waters of the most highly charged of the mineral springs. People who have had no experience in the matter beyond the sight of a run-away nag, may not "see the joke," but let such skeptics, even the most hardened, seat themselves amidst the brilliant crowd which gathers on the grand stand; let them watch the eager and the exultant eyes of all around, at the approach of the impatient steeds, and see the thickening interest as they start on their course, an interest rising into breathless, almost painful intensity as the goal is neared, and if they fail to catch the general infection, then are they stoics indeed, who had better turn hermits and eschew the weak humanities of this mortal world.

There are many good people who would not, if they could, in any way enjoy the sports and pleasures of the turf, but, on the contrary, shun them and their allurements as snares of Satan and as roads to ruin; but why this should be so we cannot say, unless upon a general principle, which might forbid the use of any goods which the gods provide, because, forsooth, they may be abused. It is true that the Race is a popular pastime, from which fact, and from the

6

manner in which it has been and is often conducted, has acquired a vulgar repute. This, however, is purely an accident, which may be easily corrected. The "betting-book," common to the excitement of the sport, may tempt to unjust gain or to unhappy loss of fortune. So indeed may, in a greater or less degree, all the chances of this chanceful world and its occupations. There are "betting-books" in Wall Street, not little pocket-editions for occasional use, but great ponderous volumes, which are poured over with grave brows from morn to eve by the worthiest folk, and every merchant's ledger is, indeed, in its way, only a "betting-book." The turf may lead to dissipations, harmful to health and due sobriety—so, too, may any gentleman's well-spread mahogany; or, may-be, a loss of precious time: but how much time is daily lost without reproof! On the whole, is it not better and wiser and braver to manfully pluck the flowers which bestrew our path, rather than to deny ourselves their sweet fragrance, in fear of being stung by some intermingled thorn or nettle?

Certain it is that the gay sport grows in favor with the growth of the popular intelligence and refinement. It is gradually passing from the control of its former rude masters into the hands of gentlemen of character and culture. Day by day it is becoming an amusement more elegant and more fashionable, and fair ladies, in all their drawing-room grace and gorgeousness, now sanctify it with their eager presence. We know, indeed, some very excellent men, whom even the worldlings reverently call reverend, who handle the ribbons with a genuine zest, and who do not despise a horse on account of his speed.

Saratoga Lake.

SARATOGA LAKE.

A trip to "the Lake" would be a pictorial necessity to all Saratoga visitors, even if it were not, as it is, the terminus of the principal and most convenient "drive" from the village, and only some five miles away.

It is a lovely water in every aspect, not grand in its characteristics, to be sure, but replete with quiet and gentle beauty. It is, too, of very commanding proportions, having a liberal length of nine miles, and a breadth, in its widest division, of nearly five miles. Many and varied scenes of beauty occur within this broad range of water and shore. The boldest feature of the lake is the elevation to be seen on the right, and familiar to visitors as "Snake Hill." It may be reached by the little steamer which plies between the Lake House and the Sulphur Spring, or by foot across the long bridge, and thence by a romantic path, which winds along the shore on the crest of a line of cedar bluffs, upon one of which is a refreshment station, known as Meyer's Lake House. The piazzas of this hotel afford an agreeable view of the lake and its surroundings.

It is said that there existed, once upon a time, a terrible lair of rattlesnakes, midway on the flank of the hill—hence its rather forbidding name. The visitor, however, may trudge fearlessly onward at this day, since St. Patrick seems to have given his careful attention to the region, and the snakes of old are now happily *non est*. It is said that there once dwelt on the hill an old fellow, whose profession it was to catch the varmints for public exposition and sale, and who at length was bitten by them and slain. But we have heard of this "old fellow" on every snake-hill or hollow which we have ever visited, and also of his untimely and inevitable end.

A more interesting, if not a more historically reliable reminiscence is an oft-quoted tradition, "scribed" to the poetry of the spot by that charming *raconteur*, N. P. Willis. "There is," he says, "an Indian superstition attached to this lake, which probably has its source in its remarkable loneliness and tranquillity. The Mohawks believed that its stillness was sacred to the Great Spirit, and that if a human voice uttered a sound upon its waters, the canoe of the offender would instantly sink. A story is told of an Englishwoman, in the early days of the first settlers, who had occasion to cross this lake with a party of Indians, who, before embarking, warned her most impressively of the spell. It was a silent, breathless day, and the canoe shot over the smooth surface of the lake like an arrow. About a mile from the shore, near the centre of the lake, the woman, willing to convince the savages of the weakness of their superstition, uttered a loud cry. The countenances of the Indians fell instantly to the deepest gloom. After a moment's pause, however, they redoubled their exertions, and in frowning silence drove the light bark like an arrow over the waters. They reached the shore in safety, and drew up the canoe, and the woman rallied the chief on his credulity. 'The Great Spirit is merciful,' answered the scornful Mohawk; 'He knows that a white woman cannot hold her tongue.'"

The lake is rich in material for piscatory sport. There was a time when it was famous for its supplies of trout; and before the building of the mills at the entrance of Fish

Creek (the outlet of the lake into the Hudson), shad and herring came up to try the water in the spring of the year. Although these fish are now to be seen no more at Saratoga, there remain other varieties hardly less attractive to the fisherman and the *gourmet*. Among them are the perch, the pickerel, the muscalonge, and the black or Oswego bass. The best locality in which to look for perch is said to be the deep water opposite Snake Hill, where they are frequently taken of the agreeable weight of three and even of four pounds. For pickerel one should try the ground at the end of the lake just above Stafford's Bridge. Near the east end of the bridge boats and bait and lines may be procured of " Uncle John " Tale, who makes it his occupation to supply these needs of the Saratoga Waltons.

When your fish is caught, you may have it cooked in marvellous style, in the cuisines of the excellent hotel on the banks of the lake, known far and near as the LAKE HOUSE, and administered by Mr. Moon, a landlord of high repute, especially in the concoction of those epicurean luxuries—game-dinners.

THE CEMETERY.

A village cemetery is always an object of as much interest to the stranger as to the resident, though from different feelings and different points of view. The one resorts to its quiet haunts to read over again the changeful chapters in. his own past life, and to recall memories of absent mates and friends ; while the other finds there curious hints and histories of the character and story of the people among

6*

whom his interests and sympathies are, for the moment,
cast. Then, too, these cells of the silent are, for the most
part, provided and preserved with generous hand and
thoughtful care, making them objects of attraction to the
eye no less than to the heart.

GLIMPSE EASTWARD FROM THE CEMETERY.

Our Saratoga cemetery is, it is true, not old enough to
have gathered within its pale many records, and few of
that striking individuality of character often to be read on

ancient and lichen-covered tombs; yet it has its tale of love and sorrow, and its annals of good and noble lives, which do honor to those who are left and to the region where they dwell. Besides what the stranger may learn in the village cemetery of Saratoga, of the character of the place—from the records he will see there of the names and deeds of her departed sons and daughters—he will find much satisfaction and pleasure in wandering through the well-ordered walks which traverse in all directions the slopes of the picturesque acres, piously devoted here to the memory of the departed ones; and in looking abroad from the more lofty portions of the ground, at the glimpses afforded here and there of the far-reaching meadows and the distant hills.

WAGMAN'S HILL.

About three miles beyond Chapman's Hill, in a general northeast course, lies the yet loftier elevation called Wagman's Hill. It offers a charming view in all directions. The western picture is made up of the blue ranges of the Kayaderosseras, and the intervening table-lands, dotted everywhere with fruitful farms and happy homesteads. In the remoter north are the yet loftier peaks of the great Adirondack range; eastward may be seen the green hills of old Vermont, and far in the south stretch the Helderberg and the Catskill cliffs. In the intervening plains may be watched the windings of the Hudson, just started on its great journey to the sea; and the small but not less lovely waters of the Mohawk, of the Kayaderosseras and Fish Creek, and many other streams and lakes and ponds of exquisite beauty, as thus seen gleaming and gloaming far off in the sunlight and shade of a soft summer eve.

Wagman's Hill is not more than seven miles from Saratoga, and presents a motive for a moderate excursion, either to commence or to close the day ; or it may be put in as a postscript, and taken pleasantly by moonlight. The return trip may be made by Stafford's Bridge and Avery's Lake House.

CHAPMAN'S HILL.

If the visitor should be at the Lake, and disposed to continue his drive, rather than to amuse himself in angling, rowing, or sailing, or in enjoying Mr. Moon's eminent hospitality, he may turn his horses' heads across the bridge, and, after following the shore for a mile or more, turn upwards to the left, when he will soon find himself high up on the eminence known as Chapman's Hill. Here he will stand one hundred and eight feet above the level of the lake, and gaze abroad upon a panorama well worth the seeing. Directly below sleep the peaceful waters, stretching their mirrowing surface over an area of twenty square miles. Looking westward, the lake shore is seen to ascend boldly to the reach of table-land above. This table-land spreads back a dozen miles to the base of the Kayaderosseras Mountains, and the mountains continue the view in fresh and varying beauties, their lofty flanks contrasting gratefully with the intervening meadows, fallow, and farms. The Kayaderosseras Hills rise some two thousand feet above the level of tide-water, and extend over a long range of fifty or sixty miles. When life at the Springs grows weary, renew it by a peep at such inspiriting scenes as this and other neighboring localities afford.

BARHYDT'S LAKE.

There is a little tarn in the grounds of Dr. Russell Childs, who lives in a pretty Italian villa upon its banks. In former days and before it fell into the possession of its present occupant, it was a place of popular resort, especially by tourists in quest of piscatorial exercise. Then, there was a tavern by the shore, where dwelt Mynheer Barhydt, a Dutchman of the most legitimate and most stolid stock. This most worthy Boniface equipped his guest with boats and bait, and whether he were successful or not in his sport, provided him a board bounteously spread with dainty and luscious trout.

LAKE LOVELY.

Not a great distance from the village, and accessible by way of Union Avenue,—a broad carriage-road, opened during the year 1866,—is an interesting sheet of water, bearing the euphonious name of Lake Lovely. Though not of very great extent, it has many points of considerable attraction, in its bold hilly shores, overrun with tangled shrubs and crowned with ancient hemlock of loftiest stature. In one of the deep glens about the lake, nearly opposite Abel's Lake House, the visitor may "call on Echo," and be answered in Echo's softest and most musical strains.

SCHUYLERVILLE.

At the point where Fish Creek, the outlet of Saratoga Lake, enters the Hudson, is the village of Schuylerville: a pleasant place, in the heart of a very interesting region. It was once the residence of General Schuyler, of Revolutionary memory, and was named in his honor.

Schuyler's homestead and all its appurtenances were destroyed by the enemy, under Burgoyne, in 1777. The memorable locality where the British commander surrendered his conquered sword to General Gates, is said to be only a little way to the northward of the site of the old Schuyler mansion.

The veteran must surely have found some consolation for his private loss, as he wandered from the ashes of his homestead to the adjoining grounds, so interesting and important in his country's history.

General Schuyler contributed much to the settlement and growth of Saratoga. In 1783 he opened a road thither from his own home at the mouth of Fish Creek, and, pitching his tent in the forest, remained there with his family during some weeks, hunting the game in the woods and drinking the water from the springs. The following year (1784) he erected a small frame-house—the first one ever built in the village, and which he occupied every summer during the rest of his life. The neighborhood should not be overlooked, as few localities in the land awaken associations of such thrilling interest in the hearts of all who delight in musing upon the by-gone trials and triumphs of their native land.

BALLSTON SPRINGS.

Ballston, once renowned for its mineral fountains—more so even than Saratoga itself—lies upon the railway route, seven miles distant, and is passed on the approach to Saratoga from Albany to Schenectady. It is situated in pleasant valley-land upon each side of a small tributary of the Kayaderosseras Creek.

The mineral waters of Ballston were known earlier than those of Saratoga; and when Sir William Johnson visited the High Rock, he went via Ballston, and was accompanied by Michael McDonald, who had settled there in 1763.

The township of Ballston was organized in 1788, and was incorporated in 1807. It is at this time the county-seat of Saratoga, and thus adds to its other attractions the possession of the public buildings of the region.

A log-house was erected for the accommodation of guests at Ballston, in 1772, which was enlarged and improved in 1790, when, the war being over, the suspended business of the settlement began to be renewed.

The first modern monster-house was erected by Nicholas Low, in 1804. This house was the present *Sans-Souci*, now three stories in height, with a length of one hundred and sixty feet, and wings of one hundred and fifty.

For a long time the mineral waters of Ballston were held in high repute, and the village grew and prospered. Soon, however, the Saratoga star began to rise above it. The Ballston waters proved difficult to secure, owing to the peculiar character of the substratum which underlies the region, and the place lost its prestige.

The most approved fountains at Ballston are the United States, the Fulton Chalybeate Spring, the Franklin Sulphur, and the Low Well, the waters of which are still used with success, though they have ceased to be bottled, as they once were. The quantity of gas in these springs and the manner of its escape is said to vary very much—sometimes rising in great force, and sometimes passing off in small particles only. On one occasion, but for a short time only, the gas rose in such force and quantity as to produce a jet several feet in height.

There are yet many who delight in Ballston as a summer-home, and in its waters as remedial agents. The Saratoga guest will find the village an agreeable place to visit, going by the rail, or making it the goal of an afternoon's ride. The neighboring brooks and ponds and the pleasant country all about are well worth exploring. The village was named in honor of the Rev. Eliphalet Ball, who established himself, at an early day, some two miles and a half to the southward.

LUZERNE.

Luzerne is a pretty hamlet, lying within reach of the lower spurs of the Adirondack, at the confluence of the Upper Hudson with the Sacandaga. It is in the neighborhood of Corinth Falls, and may be reached by the Saratoga and Lake Ontario Railway, though of course no pleasure-seeking tourist will approach it by that prosaic means.

The vicinity of Luzerne is famous as a hunting and fishing ground. Trout and pickerel abound, and partridge and woodcock are to be had for fair asking. When the game is bagged, the hospitable landlord, Mr. Rockwell, will see to it that it is served as such dainties should be served, and as only landlords themselves experts in the gentle sports of field and flood know how to do it.

Among the landscape incidents of the region is a singular-looking cone, known as Potash Kettle, which rises boldly in the foreground of a mountain picture. The Hudson may be seen here, wildly rushing over rocky ledges in its hurried race to join the scarcely less turbulent waters of the Sacandaga a little way below.

The jagged shores of the river are united by a well-conditioned bridge, and the waters are utilized for saw-mill industry.

STILES' HILL.

Stiles' Hill may be reached in a drive of a few miles along the base of the Palmerton Mountain. In the vicinity of the locality known as Eli Stiles', a remarkably interesting panorama may be obtained—a panorama revealing the varied landscape for sixty miles to the south, following the gliding course of the Hudson and the Mohawk rivers. To the eastward there may be seen the mountain ranges on the borders of the Connecticut Valley, and northward the green hills of Vermont stretch away through many a mile of peak and pass, beyond the verdant and fertile plains which lie along the shores of Lake Champlain.

To the intelligent observer the country around will recall, also, many a thrilling recollection of historic story and romance; for it is, to those who know it, all hallowed ground.

7

WARING HILL.

Taking the road towards Mount Pleasant, the tourist may, after a ride of sixteen miles, find himself on the crest of Waring Hill, a point two thousand feet above tide-water and overtopping all the other highlands around.

It is a good specific for dyspepsia, bile, or blues to bear the forehead to the fresh airs of these high latitudes, dry and pure, and sparkling with electric life. Put aside your "yellow covers," and thrust from your brain all memory of their maudlin dreams, O gauzy guest! and shake yourself into life with a spanking course over their wide-awake and health-giving reaches of valley and hill. Be assured that it will do you good, body and soul, and give you a truer notion of the relative values of ruches, ribbons, waterfalls, and Empress trails.

From Waring Hill the spectator will look down upon the villages of Saratoga, Ballston, Mechanicsville, Schuylerville, Schenectady, and Waterford, with many other less important hamlets and settlements, all interspersed and enlivened by the gleam of sunny waters. Saratoga Lake spreads its broad surface to the gaze; Ballston Lake also, and Round Lake, Owl Point, the winding ways of Fish Creek, and of the Kayaderosseras; and over and above all, the great Hudson, in all its course from the Sacandaga to the labyrinths of the distant Catskills.

HAGGERTY HILL.

Haggerty Hill is a fine eminence of about eight hundred feet above tide-water, half a mile west of Greenfield Centre.

It is six miles north of Saratoga by the plankroad leading to Luzerne, on the Hudson.

Returning, it will be pleasant to take the road east, through Greenville Centre, crossing "Meeting House Hill," St. John's Corners, and thence, by the right-hand road, over the Hewit and the Westcott hills. This itinerary will afford a very delightful ride through broad meadow-lands, watered by pretty brooks and studded with thrifty farms. The hill-points on the route will give the tourist the same fine distant mountain-passages, with more or less variation, which are to be had from other elevations around Saratoga. The glimpse eastward, bounded by the shadowy ranges of the Green Mountains, is remarkably attractive. But ride whither one may, hereabouts he cannot fail to enjoy the exercise, if the weather be fine, the roads in fair order, and the heart tuned to the melodious voices of the smiling scenes around him ; for after all, it is very true what poor Slingsby says, "that no sky is blue, no leaf is verdant—it is the heart alone that has the azure and the green." So, good reader, be careful to ride forth always with a clear conscience void of all offence, if in your musings with fair nature you would hear her "voice of gladness," feel "her smile and eloquence of beauty," and be blessed by her "mild and gentle sympathy."

CORINTH FALLS.

The cataract known as Corinth Falls is a bold passage, in the Upper Hudson, some fifteen miles north of Saratoga and one mile from the old Jessup's Landing. A long line of rapids gives admonition of the impending crash of waters, when the lately placid stream, as if preparing for the crisis before it, gathers itself into the narrow limits of fifty feet space or less, and then rushes headlong down through a gorge of one hundred and fifty feet. Reaching the goal, the floods spread forth again as if to draw breath before their next and final plunge, over a dark precipice of sixty feet. It is a noble sight even now, when the detracting hand of modern improvement has in some measure robbed it of its original beauty.

The falls may be seen to advantage from the Luzerne side of the river, by crossing at the landing and climbing to the crest of the bluff, which stands a hundred feet or more above. The village, at the old Jessup Landing, will afford all reasonable ways and means for that recuperation of the physical forces which is required occasionally even by visitors of the highest poetical natures. Roaring cataracts and gurgling brooks are each and at all times extremely enjoyable ; but the adjuncts of an appetizing sandwich and of a wee drop of bourbon, say, rarely, if ever, lessen their effect upon the imagination.

THE SARATOGA BATTLE-GROUND AT BEMIS HEIGHTS.

A visit to the scene of the great battle of Saratoga, which ended in the surrender of the British army under General Burgoyne to the Americans under Gates, will occupy a pleasant though a somewhat long day's excursion ; or the spot may be reached sooner from the Springs by the aid of the railway tending thither.

The battle was fought and won upon the elevated lands at Bemis Heights, two and a half miles from the Hudson, in the town of Stillwater, in Saratoga County. The visitor may obtain all desired information respecting the precise localities of the struggle from residents and cicerones on the grounds. At the time of the eventful Battle of Saratoga the American troops were in high feather at their successes in the defeat of St. Leger and at Stark's brilliant performance at Bennington, which had occurred during the latter part of the preceding month. The enemy's forces in the neighborhood were believed to be in a bad way generally, and all parties were ignorant of the British progress on the Hudson below and yet further south. Troops poured in from all quarters, and General Gates was in good trim for the work which soon fell to him.

As an illustration of how chance seems to rule in war, there is recorded a story, which, with a different sequel, might have entirely altered the relative fortunes of Burgoyne and Gates at that time. Clinton, the English commander on the Hudson, had despatched a messenger to Burgoyne, announcing his success and promising him relief; which message, had it but safely reached its destination, might have led to an avoidance of the fatal rencontre into which the English general was led at Saratoga. The message contained the brief words, " *nous y voici*, and nothing between us but Gates." It was enclosed in a silver bullet.

The messenger fell in with a squad of American troops, whom he unluckily mistook for friends, as they chanced just then to be arrayed in red coats, recently captured from

7*

an English storeship. He incautiously divulged his errand,
when he discovered his sad mistake, and Burgoyne lost his
saving message and the Battle of Saratoga.

The happy position of the American army on the
Heights was chosen by the Polish ally Kosciusko, who
served informally as chief engineer on the occasion. It
may be curious also to recall the fact, as we stroll over the
once gory ground, that much of the success of the day was
owing to the impetuous ardor and daring bravery of the
very Arnold who, at a later day, so wofully marred his
patriotic record at West Point. So highly did Washington
esteem Arnold's services at that time, that he bestowed upon
him, with other marks of consideration, one of three sets
of military ornaments which had been sent to him by some
person in France, " for the First of American captains, and
the two chieftains he might consider worthy to share the
compliment with him."

The great struggle occurred on the afternoon of the 7th
of October, 1777. Burgoyne was observed to be moving
his troops, with an evident inclination to work, should the
opportunity offer ; when Gates, in his turn, determined
" to indulge him," and gave order " to begin the game."
Colonel Morgan was at once despatched towards the British
right, while Poor was ordered to look after his left. Both
officers executed their commissions so effectually that, in
exactly fifty-two minutes after the first shot was fired, the
enemy beat a retreat, leaving behind two twelve and six
six-pounders, with the loss of more than four hundred
officers and men, killed, wounded, and captured, among
whom were General Frazer, Major Ackland, and Sir
Francis Cook.

Scarcely had the enemy re-entered his lines, when he was followed by General Arnold and Colonel Brooks in a furious assault upon his entire works from right to left, with such effect, that when the night put a stop to the contest, Burgoyne was glad of the opportunity to withdraw to a stronger position on the heights and nearer to the river, where he might avoid another engagement with the foe, who already possessed parts of his works, and was evidently ready to renew the attack with the returning light.

Thus ended the important action on Bemis Heights, though it was not until some time later that Burgoyne, driven to his last resource, and finding his position utterly desperate, laid down his arms and surrendered to his victorious foe.

After the decisive victory of the glorious 7th of October the spirits of the American troops rose high, and Gates threw heavy detachments higher up the river to oppose the retreat of the enemy. No attack was made; but nevertheless Burgoyne was compelled to abandon his strong post. He retreated on the night of the 10th October towards Saratoga, with the loss of his hospital and a part of his baggage and stores. Taking a new position on the Hudson, he again found himself beset by his antagonist, who was already on the opposite side, ready to dispute his passage. The British army was now surrounded by a numerically superior force, which was constantly increasing, and was flushed with success. Burgoyne's gallant array of eight thousand men had been reduced to three thousand five hundred, and his provisions were nearly exhausted. Thus circumstanced, and being surrounded by a force four times as great as his own, and with every avenue of escape closed against him, he was obliged to open a treaty with Gates, which terminated in the formal surrender of the remnant of his army.

The spot where the defeated commander gave up his sword, and which is called the " Surrender Ground," is a few miles further up the river than the battle-field.

BAKER'S FALLS.

These fine cascades are in the Hudson River, about four miles below Glen's Falls. The waters here make a descent of about seventy feet in one hundred rods, falling in a series of bold rapids, and at intervals in little picturesque and perpendicular leaps down rugged glens.

The spot may be conveniently visited in connection with Glen's Falls, in the river above, and may be reached from Saratoga by railway fifteen miles to Moreau Station, and hence by an agreeable stage-ride over pleasant hills and dales.

GLEN'S FALLS.

This remarkable passage in the waters of the Upper Hudson is about twenty miles northeast of Saratoga and on the route from the Springs to Lake George. It is a spot of great attraction, from its historical and poetical associations no less than for its natural beauty.

Here the river, but now so gentle and peaceful in its course, makes through a ravine of bold jagged rock of some nine hundred feet in length. Looking at the broad stately floods of the Hudson, nearer to the sea, one would hardly suspect it of being capable of such mad tantrums as it is led into by the tortuous crags which it here encounters. But this is the period of its youth, when it may be allowed to sow a few wild-oats. In its native aspect, before the hand of civilization robbed the wilderness of its trees, and replaced them with factory and mill, this must have been a wild, even a weird spot. The volume and the impetuous rush of the waters over the rude rocks is still a grand sight, despite the many materials of industry which obtrude themselves upon the eye, and which seem to be vainly striving to turn poetry into prose.

The spot still possessed all its primeval wilderness in the warlike days of the French and Indian incursions; and no fabrics of human art were to be seen there at the later period of the Revolution, excepting a military blockhouse here and there, or occasionally a more pretentious defence, dignified with the high-sounding name of fort.

The rushing floods were not degraded to the ignoble work of turning mills, and the marble cliffs were all unquarried, when "The Last of the Mohicans" stole with stealthy step through the wild ravines, and Cooper's gentle heroines, fair Alice and Cora Munroe, were sheltered there from the search of their treacherous foes.

It was in this neighborhood that the unfortunate Jenny McCrea was murdered by the Indians, allies of the British during the Revolution. She dwelt at the time in the lone house of an old Scotch widow, and on the night of the murder was unprotected save by the companionship of an old negro woman. In the apprehension of danger, a guard had been placed in the vicinity, but, by an odd chance, this very protection proved the poor maid's ruin. According to the story, the murdering red-men had been sent to bring her away to a place of greater security by a youth to whom she was about to be married. On their way the messengers were beset by the guard, whom they dispersed or despatched, and then afterwards falling into a dispute as to the division of the whiskey which had been promised them in reward for their good services in bringing away the hapless girl, killed her as the readiest way of settling the quarrel. Thus, by such slight mischance was Jane McCrea changed from a poor ignorant country girl into a deathless heroine of romance.

LAKE GEORGE.

As the Saratoga guest will of course avail himself of his proximity to Lake George, to visit that most beautiful resort, it is proper that we should say, in brief, what he may and what he should see there. The trip from the Springs to the Lake and back, may be done pleasantly in a couple of days, if no more time should be at command; and a more agreeable diversion cannot be imagined. Besides, Lake George *must* be seen, even at a sacrifice of convenience, being as it is the most charming place of its kind in America, if indeed it is to be surpassed anywhere in the wide world.

The distance from the Springs to the Lake is about thirty miles, fifteen of which will be travelled by rail to Moreau Station, and the rest by stage over a fine plankroad and through a very pleasant country.

Scene Eastward: on the Lake Road.

When within nine miles of the Lake the tourist will reach the village of Glen's Falls, where he may see the grand cataracts of the Upper Hudson, which we have described upon another page.

Five miles yet nearer his point of destination, he will pass, on the immediate road-side, the interesting historical ground known as the Bloody Pond. Here Colonel Williams was slain in an unfortunate encounter with the French and Indians, on the 8th of September, 1755. The victims of the disaster were rudely buried beneath the slimy waters of the pond. The ancient boulder close by is called Williams' Rock.

The first view of the Lake as we approach in this direction is surpassingly beautiful, much of the wide expanse of water coming suddenly upon the sight as we reach the crest of the bordering hills. From this point the descent to the shore is rapid; reaching which, we may halt at the village of Caldwell, or, as most people will prefer to do, continue half a mile further around the beach, to the right, and find ourselves happily at home in the elegant halls of the Fort William Henry Hotel, as pleasant a resting-place as may be found the country through.

Lake George is, from the head or southern extremity at Caldwell, to the foot or northern end, at the village of Ticonderoga, about thirty-six miles long, and may be traversed in the pretty steamers which ply the waters daily to and fro. Should the weather be propitious, nothing more delightful could be desired than this little voyage up and down the lovely waters, with their bold and ever-changing mountain shores, their innumerable islands, and their volumes of thrilling historic remembrances.

Fort William Henry Hotel stands upon hallowed ground, the site being that of old defences of the period of the French and Indian War. Near by, also, are the ruins of Fort George, which was a work of interest and importance in its day.

The fairy voyage is scarcely begun before we pass Diamond Island, which fronts Dunham Bay. It was here that Burgoyne, in 1777, established a military depot, and had a skirmish with the American troops.

To the north of Diamond Isle lies Long Island, in front of Long Point, which makes into the Lake from the east. Between the north side of this point and the mountains is Harris Bay, where Montcalm moored his boats and landed in 1767.

DOME ISLAND

lies midway between the shore, about twelve miles above Caldwell. It was a temporary shelter for Putnam and his party on their errand to General Webb, with advice of the movements of the enemy at the mouth of the Northwest Bay.

BOLTON

is a steamboat-landing in this neighborhood, which is one of the finest parts of the Lake. An excellent hotel will be found at Bolton, and a small hamlet lies at a little distance from the landing. The neighborhood is a favorite head-quarters for visitors who delight themselves in the sports of the angle, and many fine trout are still to be found here-abouts.

THE TONGUE MOUNTAIN

steps with its bold stride southward into the waters, in the neighborhood of Bolton, forming the Northwest Bay on one side, and the main passage of the Lake, called the Narrows, on the other. The Tongue is a very picturesque mountain-ridge, and goes a great way in forming the natural beauties of the Lake, dropping in as it does so admirably in many of its most striking views. It is not long since the deer was successfully hunted here, and the game may yet be found with industrious search.

SHELVING ROCK.

On the east side of the Lake and at the southern entrance to the Narrows is a semi-circular hill, faced with bold pali-sade cliffs. At the base of these rocks rattlesnakes once abounded, and may yet be found, if the chase should be interesting.

The widest part of the Lake is hereabouts; the distance from shore to shore at Bolton being from three to four miles as compared with the average breadth of two miles. The most beautiful of the many islands lie within this magic circle, and prominent among them is that curiously-shaped spot known as Ship Island.

THE NARROWS

is the contracted passage of the Lake from the bay at the lower point of the Tongue Mountain to the wider waters

8

around Sabbath-Day Point above. The hills here rise in magnificent proportions, and present stirring pictures scarcely less bold than the transit of the Hudson through the gorges of the Highlands.

THE BLACK MOUNTAIN,

lying on the east side of the Lake in its passage through the Narrows, and dividing it from the lower waters of Lake Champlain, is the loftiest of the mountain peaks, with its elevation of twenty-two hundred feet. It is stately and massive in form and extent, and of fine contour, artistically viewed, being indeed the chiefest pictorial incident of the Lake. It is itself an admirable passage in many of the pictures to be seen from the waters and shores, while from its rocky crown magnificent views may be obtained of the entire expanse of the Lake and of the country for many miles around. At the base of the mountain on the east lie the waters of Champlain, and beyond, the Vermont hills, marshalled by the lofty peaks of Mansfield and the Camel's Hump. Upon the south is the French Mountain. Lying back from the Lake and northward, with many an intervening valley and hill, are the grand peaks and ridges of the Adirondack.

It is rarely that a panoramic view is so extended and at the same time so varied in incident as that which may be seen from the crest of Black Mountain, and yet very few tourists venture upon the toil of making the somewhat rugged ascent. The enterprise, however, would scarcely fail to make an acceptable contrast to the quieter life on the peaceful shores and waters below.

SABBATH-DAY POINT

is approached as our steamer emerges from the northern end of the passage of the Narrows. The "Point" is formed by a sunny little stretch of meadow and pebbly beach, which hereabouts steps gently into the Lake, in pleasant contrast with the bolder rocky shores around it.

Sabbath-Day Point was named by General Abercrombie, in memory of his departure thence (on a Sunday morning), on his way to attack the French at Fort Ticonderoga above. The spot was the scene of a skirmish, in 1756, between the colonists and a party of French and Indians; when the latter, though much the superior force, were driven from the ground with very considerable loss.

A battle also occurred here in 1776, between a party of American militia and a force of Indians and Tories, in which the latter were repulsed with some forty or more of their number killed or wounded.

The Lake widens into a spacious bay above the Narrows, which is shut in on the north by the rocky barriers of Rogers' Slide and Anthony's Nose. On the west shore of the bay the road winds along through shady groves past Garfield's old hotel, where there is a steamboat landing and an agreeable place of sojourn—a place, at one period, of very fashionable resort.

Rogers' Slide is a ragged promontory, four hundred feet in height, which steps into the Lake face to face with Anthony's Nose, the two headlands approaching each other so nearly as to leave but a comparatively narrow passage for the waters of the bay below to that above. The pass thus formed makes a bold and pleasing picture, and is a favorite subject of the pencil. Rogers' Slide is, for the most part, a precipitous wall of rugged rock, adorned here and there with a shrub or two, and crowned with a scant covering of bushes and trees.

The tradition which accounts for the origin of the name of Roger's Slide is doubtless familiar enough to the reader; as how its gallant godfather, being once upon a time pursued to the brink of the precipice by the Indians, made his escape, as they supposed, by fearlessly sliding down the face of the granite cliff! Perhaps he did, for nobody knows, and perhaps he knew the spot well enough to descend with more safety if with less romance.

PRISONERS' ISLAND

is two miles above the pass of the Slide. This spot was a prison station of the English at the period of the Colonial War with the French and Indians. The lake-shore here loses its bold aspect, and drops down into gentle verdant slopes. The water, too, which in some parts is very deep, grows so shallow as everywhere to show the pebbles and sand beneath. This last feature was a blessing in the olden time to the captives on Prisoners' Island, as it often permitted them to evade the eyes of their officers and wade ashore.

Howe's Landing is west of Prisoners' Island. At this point there once debarked a flotilla, the like of which will never probably be again seen on the marge of these placid waters, even should the spot again become the gathering-point of contending armies.

Near by where Howe landed in years gone by, the tourist, at the present day, will also land; and, stepping into the waiting stage, will begin his overland trip of about four miles to the old fort.

TICONDEROGA,

or " Tye," as it is familiarly named in the vicinity, is a little village at the north end or foot of Lake George, on the stream which bears the waters of Horicon to those of Lake Champlain. It is a picturesque brook, this outlet of the Lake, full of charming bits of rapid and waterfall, and at its confluence with Champlain are the famous ruins of Ticonderoga—ruins unsurpassed in the wide Union for romantic effect, both in themselves and in the beauty of the spot which they adorn.

Very much of the old military wall is yet standing, enough indeed to show fully the extent and design. Seen by moonlight, with the waters of old Champlain and the bordering mountains in the mysterious background these venerable ruins are as suggestive as any castle crags on the poetic Rhine. Just below the old fort and on opposite shores of the Lake, are Mount Defiance and Mount Independence.

Ticonderoga was erected by the French in 1756, and was then called Fort Carrillon. It was naturally a place of great strength, being surrounded on three sides by water and the rear protected by an impassable swamp. Unluckily, however, General Burgoyne found a means of overcoming these considerable advantages by placing his

8*

guns upon the pinnacle of Mount Defiance, on the south side of the Lake George outlet and seven hundred and fifty feet above, from whence he sent his shot with ease and provoking certainty into the midst of the unsuspecting garrison.

Every one is familiar enough with the anecdote accompanying the capture of this work by the American troops under Ethan Allen, at the opening of the Revolutionary War; when Allen and his Green Mountain Boys surprised the commandant one fine night, and arousing him from his peaceful dreams, demanded the surrender of the place "in the name of the great Jehovah and the Continental Congress!"

From Ticonderoga the traveller may return to Saratoga through Lake George, or he may step on board one of the Champlain steamers, in their daily calls at the fort, and sail down the Lake to Whitehall, and thence speedily back to the Springs by rail.

Before we leave the neighborhood, it behooves us to speak of the pleasures to be found on the waters of Lake George, in the manly and romantic exercises of boating and fishing. For these delightful sports the means and appliances are ample.

Nothing can be pleasanter on a fine fresh summer-day, or on a soft zephyrous moonlight night, than to pull at will over the pellucid waters, landing here and there, as the beauty of the scene may tempt, upon the rocky or the pebbly shore or amidst the verdure of the countless islands. Neither can any amusement better please those who like it than the dropping of the treacherous line, and the reward it seldom fails to yield of glorious prize of trout or bass.

Lake George was poetically named, in the Indian tongue, Horicon, or the Lake of the Silvery Waters; and by the English it was, from the singular purity of the floods, sometimes called Lake Sacrament.

THE END.

www.ingramcontent.com/pod-product-compliance
Lightning Source LLC
Chambersburg PA
CBHW032156010726
47493CB00008BA/2713